04383594

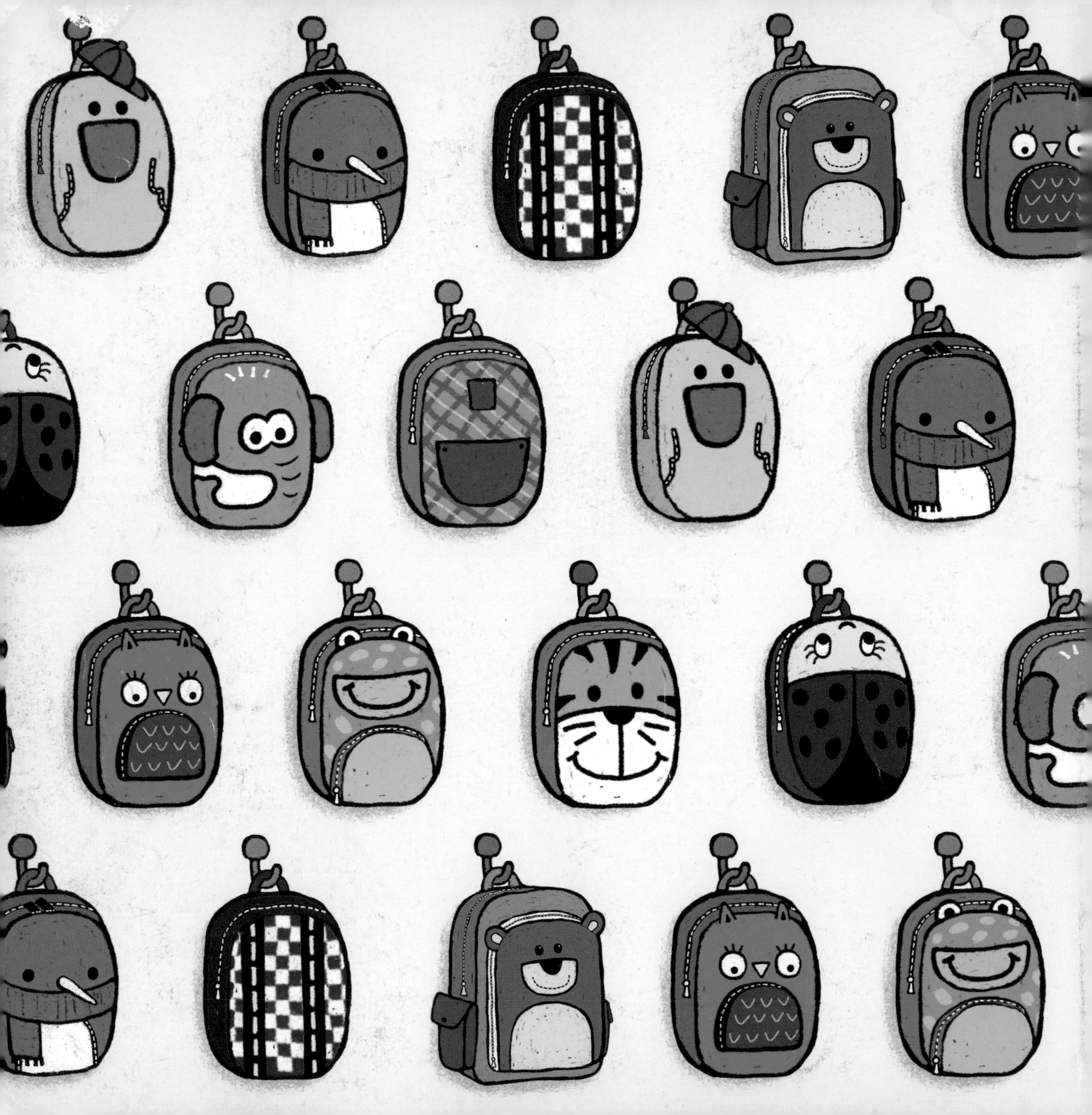

For Nicole and Jason

Bloomsbury Publishing, London, Oxford, New York, New Delhi and Sydney

First published in the United States of America in 2016
by Bloomsbury Children's Books
1385 Broadway, New York, New York 10018

This edition first published in Great Britain in 2016 by Bloomsbury Publishing Plc
50 Bedford Square, London WC1B 3DP

A CIP catalogue record for this book is available from the British Library

ISBN 978 1 4088 7979 5

Printed in China by Leo Paper Products, Heshan, Guangdong

1 3 5 7 9 10 8 6 4 2

www.bloomsbury.com

BEAR'S BIG DAY

Salina Yoon

BLOOMSBURY

LONDON OXFORD NEW YORK NEW DELHI SYDNEY

It was Bear's big day.
"I can cut my pancakes all by myself,"
said Bear. "I'm a big bear now."

"Yes, you are!" said Mama.

Mama gave him a big-bear backpack.

It had pockets for each of his things.

Lunch box

Glue

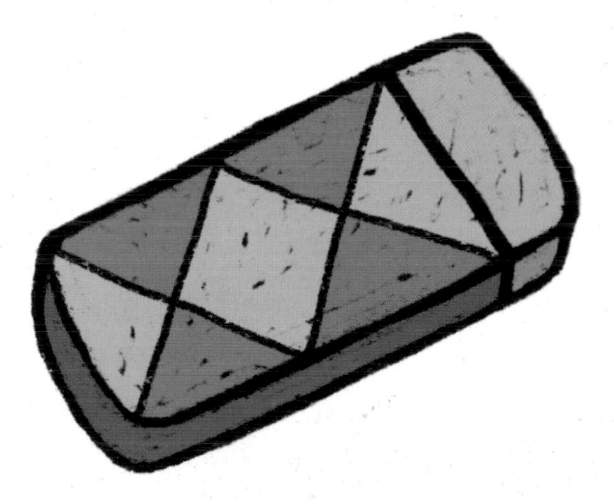

Pencil case

Crayons

Bear hugged Floppy goodbye.
"You need to stay at home," said Bear. "That's what little bunnies do. Big bears go to school."

"I love you, Floppy!"

At school, Bear met his new teacher.

“Welcome to my class,” said Miss Fox.

Bear thought school would be lots of fun.
But something – or someone – was missing.

During arts and crafts time,
everyone coloured but Bear.

At snack time, everyone ate but Bear.

At nap time, everyone slept but Bear.

Z Z Z

“What is the matter, Bear?” asked Miss Fox.
“You haven’t coloured, eaten or napped!”

"I miss Floppy," said Bear.
"I thought I was ready for school.
I guess I'm not a big bear after all."

"You ARE a big bear! Being big doesn't mean you have to do everything by yourself," said Miss Fox.

"Even big teachers need help sometimes."

Bear thought about Floppy at home alone.
Then he had an idea.

He asked Miss Fox for help.

Miss Fox pulled out some supplies,
and together they cut, glued and coloured.

After school, Bear was happy to see Floppy.

“Floppy, I made something special for you. Now I’m really ready for school!”

The next day at school . . .
Hi, friends!

Bear!
Hello!
Hi!

Bear had a wonderful time doing big-bear things.

Higher!

So did Floppy.

flower

1 + 1 = 2